Tom looked at the Hall. It was an enormous jumble of roofs, with doors and balconies in unexpected places. All the windows seemed to be of different shapes and sizes, the turrets and pinnacles and belfries sprouted in every direction. It was the sort of house that looked like a ruin even though it wasn't.

"Is it haunted?" Tom asked.

Old Barney cackled and said, "No, lad. There's no ghosts at Hemlock. Never have been and never will be, if you want my opinion. They'd scare themselves to death in there."

But Tom wasn't convinced. And when the new owners open Hemlock Hall to the public, they are determined that if the public want ghosts, then ghosts there will be . . .

BY MYSELF books are specially selected
to be suitable for beginner readers. Other
BY MYSELF books available from
Young Corgi Books include:

THE HAUNTING OF HEMLOCK HALL

Lance Salway

Illustrated by Cathie Shuttleworth

YOUNG CORGI

THE HAUNTING OF HEMLOCK HALL
A YOUNG CORGI BOOK   0 552 52416 6

Originally published in Great Britain in 1984 by
Julia MacRae Books

PRINTING HISTORY
Young Corgi edition published 1987
Reprinted 1988 (twice)

This book is set in 14/18 pt Century Schoolbook
by Colset Private Limited, Singapore.

Young Corgi Books are published by Transworld Publishers
Ltd., 61-63 Uxbridge Road, Ealing, London W5 5SA, in
Australia by Transworld Publishers (Australia) Pty. Ltd.,
15-23 Helles Avenue, Moorebank, NSW 2170, and in New
Zealand by Transworld Publishers (N.Z.) Ltd., Cnr.
Moselle and Waipareira Avenues, Henderson, Auckland.

Made and printed in Great Britain by
The Guernsey Press Co. Ltd., Guernsey, Channel Islands.

The Haunting of
Hemlock Hall

Chapter One

When Tom Pepperday first saw Hemlock Hall, he couldn't believe his eyes. For one thing, it was the biggest house he had ever seen in his life. And for another, it was the ugliest. It also looked as though it might collapse at any moment, and that only the ivy on the walls was holding the place together.

Tom turned to old Barney Larkin, the gardener, and said, 'Who lives there?'

'No one,' said Barney. 'Leastways, no one most of the time. Old Miss Hemlock, she do come down from London now and then to look things over and see what's what. Otherwise it be just Mrs Larkin seeing to the inside and me seeing to the outside.' He paused, and stared suspiciously at Tom before adding, 'And now there's you to help with the heavy work and bending. For the summer, like.'

Tom looked at the Hall again. It was an enormous jumble of gables and roofs, with doors and balconies in unexpected places. All the windows seemed to be of different shapes and sizes, and turrets and pinnacles and belfries sprouted in every direction. It was the sort of house that looked like a ruin even though it wasn't.

'Is it haunted?' Tom asked.

Old Barney cackled and said, 'No, lad. There's no ghosts at Hemlock. Never have been and never will be, if you want my opinion. They'd scare themselves to death in there.' He cackled again and spat accurately into a lavender bush.

Tom was disappointed. He had hoped for ghosts. He could just imagine headless skeletons floating in and out of the windows, and terrifying screams echoing across the lawns at dead of night. Hemlock Hall *looked* like a haunted house.

'No ghosts at all?' he persisted. 'Are you sure?'

'Sure as I know those borders need weeding,' Barney said firmly. 'Get on with it, lad, and forget about ghosts. There's no ghosts at Hemlock.'

But Tom wasn't convinced. He had spent all his life in the nearby village of Much Hemlock, and for as long as he could remember there had been stories about ghosts at Hemlock Hall. Tom had never seen the house until he came to work in the gardens because it lay a long way from the road and the big gates only opened two or three times a year to admit old Miss Hemlock's battered Bentley. But, now that he had seen the Hall for himself, Tom found it hard to believe that the place wasn't haunted.

And who could blame him? If ever a house deserved to be haunted, it was Hemlock Hall. Not only was it very ugly but it was also extremely ancient. It was no one's fault that the house was old (unless you blamed Oliver Cromwell for *not* burning it down during the Civil War) but the fact that it was ugly was entirely the fault of Admiral Sir Humphrey Hemlock.

Sir Humphrey had inherited the Hall from his father a hundred years before, and he'd lived there with his wife and daughters – when he wasn't away at sea, that is. Each time he returned from a voyage, the Admiral would find a new daughter waiting for him and then, by way of celebration, he would add a few more rooms to the house, or else a tower and a gargoyle or two. By the time he died, Sir Humphrey had accumulated an enormous ugly house and eleven enormous ugly daughters.

Most of the daughters married and left home (they may have been enormous and ugly but they were also very rich) but Hemlock Hall stayed where it was, a very large blot on the Dorset landscape. Earlier Hemlocks had added bits to the house over the years (a Tudor hall here, a Georgian portico there, Regency verandahs everywhere) but these humble extensions were dwarfed by the changes that Sir Humphrey made. He added Oriental domes and minarets, Gothic cloisters and towers, and an entire wing built to resemble an Austrian castle. He pulled down the old stable block and built a new one that looked like a Greek temple, and added a new kitchen in the shape of a Chinese pagoda.

Sir Humphrey didn't forget the gardens, either. The lawns and shrubberies were scattered with ugly statues and elaborate fountains and obelisks that Sir Humphrey had brought home from Egypt. A maze of yew was planted next to the kitchen garden, and a summer house in the shape of a ruined chapel was built near the lake.

As soon as Sir Humphrey had transformed Hemlock Hall into the most unpleasant house in the country, he and his long-suffering wife and his enormous ugly daughters died one by one until only the youngest daughter, Albania, was left. (Sir Humphrey had named each of his daughters after countries he had visited on his travels.) Miss Albania Hemlock refused to live at Hemlock Hall (for which she could not be blamed) but left the house in the care of Barney Larkin

and his wife, and went to live in London instead. Every now and then, Miss Hemlock would visit the Hall to make sure that most of it was still standing, but she never stayed very long.

As the years passed, Miss Albania and Barney and Hemlock Hall grew old together. By the time Tom Pepperday came to work there, the house and grounds were becoming too much for Barney and his wife to manage on their own. The lawns were shaggy and overgrown, the paths and flowerbeds were choked with weeds, and the lake was green and stagnant. The house was beginning to crumble, too. Every now and then chunks of stone would fall to the ground, and balconies and turrets would collapse without warning. Old Barney narrowly escaped death one day when an entire chimney stack crashed into the shrubbery where he was working.

No, young Tom Pepperday couldn't be blamed for thinking that the house was haunted. But, as old Barney had said, there were no ghosts at Hemlock Hall. No ghosts at all. Or were there?

Chapter Two

It was on a bright Monday morning
that the news came. Tom was busy
clipping a hedge in the rose garden
when he heard a shout behind him. He
turned, and saw old Barney waving
from the kitchen door.

'Tom! Tom!' he called. 'Come here,
lad. There's a letter!'

Tom put down his shears and ran

towards the house. Something important must have happened; Mrs Larkin only allowed him into the kitchen when it was raining, and then only for the time it took to swallow a mug of hot tea. But it wasn't raining today. And it was too early for tea.

He came to a breathless halt in the kitchen. Mrs Larkin was sitting at the scrubbed pine table, looking excited. Barney was standing beside her with a letter in his hand.

'Ah, there you be,' he said. 'There's a letter. From the lawyer in London. You'm best know about it.'

Tom looked at him blankly. He wasn't sure what a lawyer was.

'There's news,' Barney went on. 'Old Miss Hemlock's died. Ninety-two she was, though you wouldn't have believed it to look at her.'

'Oh,' said Tom. He didn't know whether to feel sorry or not.

'The last of Sir Humphrey's daughters,' Mrs Larkin sniffed. 'The end of an era.'

Tom knew all about Admiral Sir Humphrey Hemlock. In one of her more generous moods, Mrs Larkin had taken him to the dusty drawing room and shown him a dim portrait of a bearded man in naval uniform, clutching a telescope as if his life depended upon it.

'But – but what'll happen to *us*?'

Tom asked. 'What'll happen to Hemlock Hall?'

'Now that's just what this letter is all about,' Barney said. 'It seems that Miss Albania has left the property to her sister's son, Miss Bolivia Hemlock that was. *Her* son has the house now. Lives in the north somewhere, making zip fasteners for a living.'

Mrs Larkin snorted loudly. 'Funny occupation for a gentleman, if you ask me. Making zip fasteners.'

'Well, someone's got to make 'em,' Barney said. 'Can't do without 'em, can we?' And he winked at Tom.

'You used to manage perfectly well with buttons, as I recall,' Mrs Larkin said primly. 'Anyway, I don't hold with these modern inventions.'

Old Barney wisely decided to ignore her. He turned to Tom and said, 'This Mr Trotter . . . '

'Trotter?' Mrs Larkin looked as

though she couldn't believe her ears.

That's the gentleman's name,' Barney explained. 'Mr Trotter's coming down to see the Hall as soon as he can.'

'When?' Mrs Larkin asked.

Barney looked at the letter. 'The sixteenth,' he said. 'So we'll have time . . .'

'The *sixteenth*?' Mrs Larkin screeched.

'That's right,' Barney said. 'It says . . .'

'But that's today!' Mrs Larkin shouted. *'Today's* the sixteenth!'

And then, as if to prove just how right she was, they all heard the sound of a car hooting impatiently in the distance.

'Oh no!' Barney moaned. 'It must be them. Waiting for someone to open the gates.' And he rushed out of the kitchen.

Mrs Larkin screeched again and started to run round the room like a startled chicken. 'They'll want tea, and the house is a mess, and I've not made a cake, and I've nothing to wear, and . . .'

Tom slipped quietly away, leaving her to panic on her own. He walked round to the front of the house and was just in time to see a large grey Rolls-Royce purr to a halt at the foot

of the steps which led up to the entrance. Then he ducked out of sight behind a crumbling pillar as the car doors opened and the Trotter family stepped blinking into the sunshine.

There were four of them altogether: a mother and father and two children, a boy and a girl. They stood in silence for a moment or two, gazing open-mouthed at the house, and this gave Tom a chance to inspect them properly. He wasn't impressed with what he saw. The Trotters were pale and flabby and sullen, and they huddled together on the drive like four bad-tempered marshmallows. But their voices weren't pale and flabby. As soon as the Trotters opened their mouths, Tom realised with a sinking heart that the peace of Hemlock Hall would be shattered for ever.

'What a dump!' the girl said. 'Let's go home.'

'Oh, do keep quiet, Rosie,' her mother said wearily. 'You've done nothing but complain ever since we left home.'

'*This* is home now,' Mr Trotter said, 'so you'd better get used to it. And stop *whining*, you great lollop.'

Rosie Trotter scowled, and kicked a pillar at the bottom of the steps. There was a stone urn on top of it, filled with an unhappy mixture of tulips and dandelions. It began to wobble dangerously, and Tom shut his eyes. He felt sure that the urn was going to fall. He was right. There was a loud crash and, when he opened his eyes again, the urn was lying in pieces on the gravel.

'Now look what you've done!' Mr Trotter shouted.

'How was I to know it would fall?' Rosie asked reasonably. 'Stupid old house.'

'Wasn't her fault,' her brother said. He looked about twelve years old, the same age as Tom. He was just as pale and flabby as his sister, but his voice was even louder.

By now old Barney had joined them, out of breath from the long walk back from the gates.

'Ah, you must be Larkin,' Mr Trotter said when he saw him. 'Right then. Let's take a look at this place. We'll see the grounds first.'

Tom followed at a safe distance as Barney led an ungainly procession of Trotters on a conducted tour of Hemlock Hall. Mr Trotter seemed very interested in everything he saw: he admired the overgrown rose garden and the weed-infested lake and the tumbledown grottos; he praised the long gravel walks and the dried-up water garden and the dilapidated sundials; he even liked the ornamental fountains and the crumbling statues and the decrepit follies that dotted the unkempt lawns. The other Trotters were less impressed. Mrs Trotter kept complaining about her feet, and Rosie and her horrible

28

brother, Rupert, complained about each other. By the time the procession returned to the house, everyone but Mr Trotter was in a bad temper.

'It's got possibilities,' he said thoughtfully. 'Yes, it's certainly got possibilities.'

'What d'you mean, Dad?' Rupert asked.

'I'm going to open the place to the public,' Mr Trotter said.

There was a stunned silence. Tom, back in his hiding place behind a pillar, could hardly believe his ears.

'You're not serious?' said Mrs Trotter.

'Oh yes I am,' Mr Trotter replied. 'We'll tidy the place up a bit and have the public in at a pound a time.'

'But there's nothing for them to *see*,' Rosie Trotter whined.

'Not yet there isn't,' Mr Trotter said. 'But there will be. Oh yes, there will be. I've got great plans for Hemlock Hall.'

Old Barney stepped forward then. 'Begging your pardon, sir,' he said anxiously. 'But what plans would they be, now?'

A crafty smile spread across Mr Trotter's pale face. 'Just you wait and see,' he said. 'You won't recognise the old place by the time I've finished with it. Just you wait and see.'

Chapter Three

They didn't have long to wait. When Tom arrived at the hall the next morning, the place was already alive with workmen. Lorries and bulldozers blocked the drive, and the sound of drilling and banging and hammering filled the air. Old Barney and Tom carried on with their gardening as best they could, but Mrs Larkin spent

the day making endless cups of tea for the workmen. From time to time, Tom caught sight of Mr Trotter busily supervising the alterations. Rosie and Rupert Trotter amused themselves – but no one else – by getting in everyone's way.

As the weeks passed and Hemlock Hall began to change out of all recognition, old Barney grew steadily more depressed. 'It's not right,' he said, shaking his head. 'It's not right at all.

They've dug up the kitchen garden now. All my lovely cauliflowers and beans have gone. The rose garden, too. And look what they're doing to the south lawn!'

Tom looked. The south lawn was now a stretch of bare gravel, with a large sign nearby which read: CAR PARK. A children's playground occupied the kitchen garden, and gleaming roundabouts and swings and climbing frames stood where old Barney's asparagus and purple sprouting broccoli had flourished. A fun fair had been built on the site of the rose garden, and dodgem cars and a ghost train bloomed there instead. The summer houses and follies that dotted the grounds had been cunningly converted into hot dog stands and ice cream stalls, and the ruined chapel by the lake now bore a discreet label which read: GENTLEMEN.

Exactly two months after the Trotters had arrived at the house, the grand opening of The Hemlock Hall Stately Home and Amusement Park took place. Mr Trotter had managed to persuade a glamorous television star called Roxy Trent to perform the opening ceremony, and newspaper reporters and television cameras were also there to record the event for posterity. And then old Barney opened the gates to allow in the first paying customers.

In the weeks that followed, people flocked to Hemlock Hall in their hundreds. Each day the car park that had once been the south lawn was filled with cars and coaches, and old Barney (who was now in charge of parking) spent most of his time directing traffic. Tom was kept busy selling postcards and tea towels in the souvenir shop near the kitchen. From there he

could keep an eye on the people who
thronged the maze and the fun fair
and the paddling pool. He soon got
used to the constant noise of the
crowds and the roar of speedboats on
the lake, and he even learned to toler-
ate the shrill shrieks which came from
the video games in the orangery and
the loud music from the stables,
which were called The Tudor Disco.
But he knew he would never get used

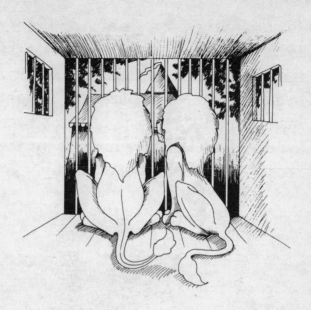

to the mournful roaring of the sad lions who occupied the zoo near the orchard, and he knew he would always hate clearing up the litter that the visitors left behind.

Inside Hemlock Hall itself, Mrs Larkin was in charge of Teas and Light Refreshments in the conservatory, and other ladies from the village had been enlisted to escort visitors round the house. There they were able

38

to admire the portrait of Admiral Sir Humphrey Hemlock with his telescope, and to inspect the four-poster bed in which Queen Elizabeth I might have slept if her visit had not been cancelled at the last minute by the arrival of the Spanish Armada.

'It's not right,' old Barney said to Tom one evening after the visitors had left. 'It's not right to ruin the old house this way. It's not right at all.'

They were trying to repair a large hole made in one of the maze hedges by a desperate tourist who had been trapped in the middle.

'And the mess they leave behind!' Tom said. 'The lily pond was fair clogged with crisp packets today.'

Barney shook his head, and they worked in silence for a while. And then Tom saw Mr Trotter heading towards them, closely followed by Rosie and Rupert.

'Ah, there you are, Larkin,' Mr Trotter bellowed. 'Just the man I want to see.'

'Yes, sir,' Barney said. 'What can I do for you?'

Tom stopped work to listen but started again when Rosie Trotter scowled and put out her tongue at him.

'Everything's going very smoothly,' Mr Trotter said. 'The public like the place. Especially the house.'

'And so they should,' old Barney said fiercely. 'It's a good old house. A bit of a hotch-potch in the building, maybe, but it's a good house all the same.'

Mr Trotter waved a dismissive hand. 'Yes, yes, I know all that. But people keep asking about ghosts. They keep asking where the ghosts are. Who they are. And where the haunted room is.'

There was silence. Tom didn't dare look at Barney.

Then, 'There's no ghosts at Hemlock Hall,' the old man said. 'None at all. Never have been and never will be.'

'Are you sure?' asked Mr Trotter.

'There *must* be ghosts!' wailed

Rosie. 'All old houses are haunted.'

'Well, this one isn't and that's that,' Barney said.

Mr Trotter looked thoughtful. 'But people are interested in the ghosts,' he said slowly. 'They want to *see* ghosts.'

'Then they'll have to go somewhere else,' said Barney. 'Tell 'em to go to Longleat.'

'But we want them to come *here*, don't we, Dad?' whined Rupert.

'That's right, son, we do. And if it's ghosts they want, then we'll *give* 'em ghosts!'

Rosie gaped at her father. 'What do you mean?' she asked.

Mr Trotter smiled at her. 'As from tomorrow, Hemlock Hall is haunted.'

Tom and Barney looked at each other. Then the old man said, 'But I've told you, sir. There's no ghosts at Hemlock Hall.'

'That's what *you* think,' said Mr Trotter mysteriously, and he turned on his heel and walked thoughtfully away, closely followed by his children.

'What's he plotting now?' Barney said, as he watched the Trotters go. 'I don't like the sound of this one bit.'

'Don't worry,' said Tom. 'I expect we'll find out soon enough.'

SEE THE
MYSTERIOUS HAUNTED
BEDROOM
AND WATCH THE
GHOSTS WALK!

50p EXTRA

Chapter Four

And they did. The next morning, a brand-new notice appeared on the gates of Hemlock Hall which read; *See the Mysterious Haunted Bedroom and Watch the Ghosts Walk. 50p extra.*

'Huh!' Tom muttered when he saw it. 'I'm not paying *that* to see ghosts that don't exist.' Instead, he went and spoke very politely to Mrs Larkin, who smuggled him into the house free of charge with the first party of visitors.

Tom had been on the conducted tour before, of course, and so he had already seen the portrait of Admiral Sir Humphrey Hemlock with his telescope, and the bed that Queen Elizabeth I had almost slept in. All he wanted to see now was the Mysterious Haunted Bedroom but he had to wait until the end of the tour for that.

Then, instead of going down the main staircase and out into the gardens, the guide led the party up a small flight of stairs that Tom had never seen before.

'We are now going into the Haunted Bedroom,' the guide said, trying to sound sinister. Tom wasn't impressed; the guide was little Miss Beech whose mother ran the post office in the village. She wouldn't have recognised a real ghost if it had hit her over the head.

Miss Beech opened a door at the top of the stairs and ushered the visitors into a dimly lit room which contained an enormous four-poster bed and three large wardrobes.

'This is the Haunted Bedroom,' Miss Beech announced dramatically. 'Anyone with a weak heart or a nervous disposition is advised to wait outside.'

None of the visitors moved. Instead, they all waited patiently in the gloom for something to happen.

'Where's the ghost then?' a fat woman said impatiently after a while. 'I'm dying for a cup of tea.'

'I'm sure the ghosts will be here soon,' Miss Beech said sweetly and then, when nothing happened, she raised her voice and said again, 'I'm *sure* the ghosts will be here *soon*.'

There was silence and then Tom heard a scrabbling noise from the bed and a muffled giggle. And then a shadowy figure crawled into view and stood up. The shape was white and plump, and there was a luminous skull where the head ought to be.

'Whoo!' screeched the shape. 'Whoo! I'm a ghost!'

Then another figure appeared from behind the door. It too was covered in what looked like a white sheet, and it

waved its arms dramatically before saying in muffled tones, 'I'm the headless hag. Beware!'

Tom, who knew at once that the headless hag was Rosie Trotter with a sheet over her head, had difficulty hiding his laughter. But the other visitors weren't at all amused.

'Those aren't ghosts!' a man said angrily.

'It's just kids mucking about. And

you charged extra for that? It's daylight robbery. I'm going to get my money back.' And he stormed out of the room. The other visitors followed him, leaving Miss Beech and the ghosts gaping at each other in the gloom.

'So much for the ghosts of Hemlock Hall,' old Barney said when Tom told him what had happened. 'Mebbe they'll forget all about it now.'

But the Trotters didn't give up as easily as that. All that day, and the next, visitors were conducted to the Haunted Room. But each time the ghosts appeared, the visitors stormed out in disgust and demanded their money back.

On the third day, Rupert and Rosie took up their places as usual in the darkened room to await the arrival of the first conducted tour.

'I'm getting fed up with this,' Rosie

muttered from behind the door. 'I can't breathe properly under this sheet. I wish I wasn't a headless hag.'

'It was *your* idea,' Rupert snapped. 'And anyway, it's not all that marvellous being a screaming skull, believe me.'

'It would help if you were a better screamer,' Rosie said nastily. 'You're about as frightening as a bread pudding.'

'And I don't know why you bother to put that sheet over your head,' Rupert said. 'You're ugly enough without it.'

Rosie was just about to reply when she heard a sudden noise on the other side of the room. 'What's that?' she asked nervously.

'What's what? I didn't hear anything.'

'There was a noise,' she said. 'Over there, by that wardrobe. A sort of – a sort of scuffling. As if someone . . . '

'You're imagining things,' Rupert said scornfully. 'There's nothing there.'

And then he, too, heard a noise. A scraping, scratching sound. And then hoarse, heavy breathing.

'Wha – what is it?' quavered Rosie. There's something there! There *is*!'

'No, there isn't,' Rupert said. But he wasn't sure any more. He wasn't sure at all.

The scraping noise grew louder and closer. Rupert stared into the shadows, straining to see if there was anything else in the room. And then the noise stopped, and there was silence.

'Told you so,' Rupert said. 'There's nothing there. Nothing at . . .'

And then he screamed in terror as a sudden grey shape loomed up in front of him, swaying and screeching. But it wasn't the shape that frightened

Rupert so much, or the horrifying
noise that it made; it was the face, the
huge green face with red staring eyes
and long yellow teeth that came closer
and closer and closer . . .

Rosie and Rupert didn't wait to see
any more. They ran to the door, flung
it open, and dashed down the stairs,
screaming as loudly as they could.

It was a pity that the staircase was so narrow. If the stairs had been wider then Rosie and Rupert would not have collided with little Miss Beech and her conducted tour who were climbing up. As it was, Miss Beech and the visitors lost their balance and tumbled back down the stairs with Rosie and Rupert on top of them. Yes, it was a pity that the staircase was so narrow.

Chapter Five

When Tom arrived for work the next
day, he saw that the notice advertis-
ing the mysterious Haunted Bedroom
had been taken down from the main
gate. He wasn't surprised. The entire
village of Much Hemlock was buzzing
with gossip about the so-called ghosts
of Hemlock Hall. Little Miss Beech
was particularly angry; she had

broken her ankle when she fell downstairs and considered this a high price to pay for being a guide at Hemlock Hall. She had also announced that she intended to strangle Rosie and Rupert Trotter as soon as she was able to lay hands on them.

Hemlock Hall seemed strangely deserted that day. Rosie and Rupert were nowhere to be found, and there were fewer visitors than usual.

'Word must have got round,'

Barney said when he and Tom met at lunch time. 'People don't like being fooled. Not by children pretending to be ghosts. People don't like it at all.'

It seemed as though Barney could be right. In the days that followed, the number of visitors dwindled steadily until, a week later, no one was coming to the house at all.

'I don't understand it,' Mr Trotter said gloomily to Barney and Tom one day. 'I'm losing money hand over fist. No one's coming to see the place and my children won't set foot here any more because they say they've seen a real ghost. A lot of nonsense, if you ask me.'

And then, two days after that, a new sign appeared on the main gates: CLOSED UNTIL FURTHER NOTICE.

Tom ran to find Barney as soon as he saw the announcement. The old man was looking happier than he had done for weeks.

'What's happening?' Tom asked. 'Is the house being closed? Are the Trotters leaving?'

'Yes and yes, lad,' old Barney said happily. 'Mr Trotter's just been down to tell me. He's closed the house down and is going back north with his family when he's sold off all the amusements.'

'So the house will be left in peace again.' Tom said.

Barney puffed contentedly on his pipe.

'That's right, lad, just as it was before. Oh, it won't be quite the same, of course, but grass'll soon grow over that car park and I can plant vegetables and roses once again.'

'Will Mr Trotter sell the place?' Tom asked.

'I expect so. If he can find anyone to buy it. But we'll cross that bridge when we come to it.'

Mrs Larkin joined them then with mugs of tea, and they sat in silence for a while, enjoying the sunshine.

'There's one thing I don't understand,' Barney said after a while. 'Young Rosie and Rupert saw a ghost in the house. A real ghost, they said.

They saw a ghost when they were play-acting. And it must be true because they were so frightened. But, I dunno, I've never heard tell of haunting here before.' And he shook his head slowly.

Tom smiled to himself and then reached into his jacket pocket. He pulled something out and handed it to Barney.

The old man looked at it for a moment and then smiled. It was a mask, a horrifying green rubber mask

with red staring eyes and long yellow teeth.

'So it was you,' he chuckled. '*You* were the ghost. It was you all the time.'

Tom nodded, and quickly stuffed the mask back in his pocket.

'Well, you've done the place a good turn,' Barney said. 'You've saved Hemlock Hall. We ought to be grateful. *All* of us.'

Before he went home, Tom decided to take a walk through the house. He wanted to enjoy the peace and quiet of the deserted rooms now that the crowds of visitors had gone, never to return.

The house seemed warm and friendly that evening. Woodwork and brass gleamed in the late evening sun, and the air was filled with the scent of roses and lavender. A bee buzzed lazily on the window-sill of the room where Queen Elizabeth I might have slept, but otherwise the house was silent.

Tom paused in the hall to take a last look round before going home. And then he saw it. A bearded man in naval uniform was standing on the stairs. He was clutching a telescope as though his life depended upon it, and he was looking straight at Tom.

Then, to Tom's amazement, the man smiled at him, and winked. A long slow wink. And then faded like smoke into the silence.